Flounder's Gift

By Rebecca Bondor
Illustrated by Jose Cardona

A Golden Book • New York

Western Publishing Company, Inc., Racine, Wisconsin 53404

It was a special day in the undersea kingdom. It was Ariel's birthday. Everyone was busy helping with the birthday party.

"I can't wait until all of my friends are here," Ariel said to her father, King Triton.

"Do you have a gift, Flounder?" asked King Triton.

"Ariel's my best friend and I want to get her the perfect gift. But I haven't found one yet," answered Flounder.

"You'd better hurry," King Triton said. "The birthday party begins very soon."

"I know, I know," said Flounder as he went to find Sebastian.

"I need your help, Sebastian," said Flounder. "Everyone has a gift for Ariel except me."

"Oh, man, this is serious," Sebastian said. "Maybe Scuttle can help."

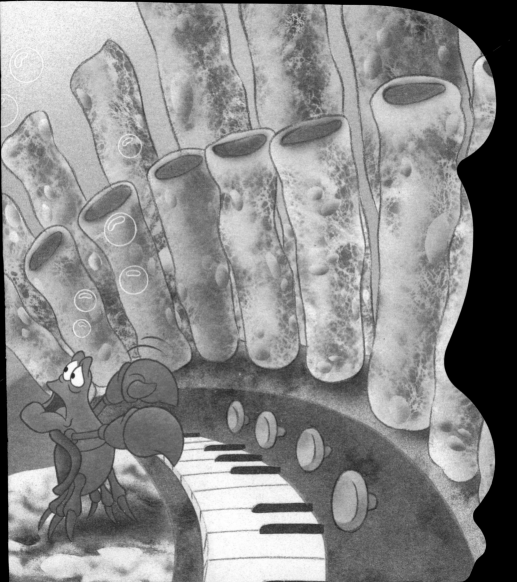

Flounder and Sebastian found Scuttle.
"Flounder is looking for a gift to give to
Ariel," explained Sebastian.
Scuttle showed them an old boot.
"Sebastian, try this baby on," suggested
Scuttle.

"Ariel will look ridiculous in this thing," complained Sebastian. "Take this off me right now!"

Luckily, Scuttle had another idea.
"Right over here is a sunken treasure,"
said Scuttle. "I'm sure you'll find something
for Ariel."

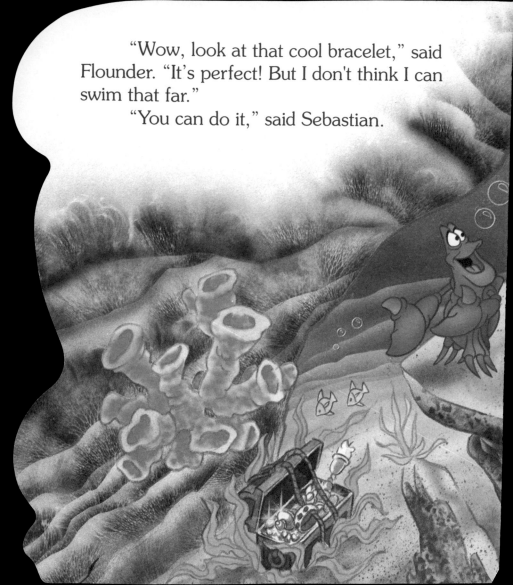

"Wow, look at that cool bracelet," said Flounder. "It's perfect! But I don't think I can swim that far."

"You can do it," said Sebastian.

"Here goes!" said Flounder. He shut his eyes tight and swam as fast as he could toward the treasure chest.

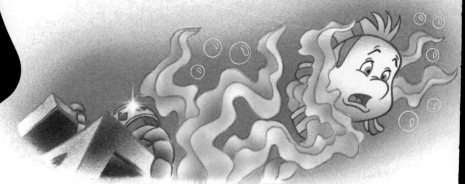

"Help!" cried Flounder. "Sea monsters are holding me prisoner."

"It's just a little seaweed," explained Sebastian.

Flounder raced toward the treasure chest again.

"Oh, no," Flounder said with a gasp. "I've been nailed by a hammerhead shark."

"There are no sharks here," Sebastian said impatiently. "You just bumped into a coral reef."

Finally Flounder swam all the way to the sunken treasure.

"Uh-oh," said Flounder. "The bracelet is caught in a rope." Flounder tugged at the bracelet, but he couldn't get it free.

"Don't forget about my claws," bragged Sebastian. "I can use my sharp claws to cut through the rope."

"Hooray! We did it!" shouted Flounder.

Flounder and Sebastian hurried back to the undersea palace.

On their way back, Flounder and
Sebastian saw Scuttle.

"Wow, those gems are flashier than
King Triton's crown!" exclaimed Scuttle.
"King Triton would have a fit if he saw that
human bracelet."

"Oh, no!" exclaimed Flounder. "I guess
I'll have to go to the party empty-finned."

Flounder and Sebastian arrived just in time for the party.

"Happy birthday, Ariel," said Sebastian as he played the concerto he had composed for Ariel's birthday.

"I'm so sorry, Ariel," said Flounder sadly. "I tried to get you the perfect gift, but I couldn't find one."

Ariel gently put her arm around Flounder.

"Having you as my best friend is the perfect gift," said Ariel.